Mary F. Waterbury

Light for Little Ones

Mary F. Waterbury

Light for Little Ones

ISBN/EAN: 9783337249274

Printed in Europe, USA, Canada, Australia, Japan

Cover: Foto ©Andreas Hilbeck / pixelio.de

More available books at **www.hansebooks.com**

LIGHT

FOR

LITTLE ONES.

BY

MARY F. WATERBURY.

PORTLAND:

HOYT, FOGG AND BREED.

1872.

CONTENTS.

CHAPTER I.

FRANKIE AND HIS HOME.

FRANKIE's home was on the bank of a large creek, the Kayaderossevass. Its water turned the great wheels of many a mill and factory. These mills were long, high buildings, filled with windows, and having steep, dusty, narrow stairways. The water was clear and blue when it flowed by Frankie's home, but after that it went foaming and dashing over the dam, and seemed intent upon doing as much work, and making as much noise as it could. It made the wheels whirl around, and they started the machinery in the mills, and then for a buzz and whirr and roar all day long!

The house in which Frankie lived was white,

with a piazza across the front covered with trumpet honey-suckles—those bright red flowers, shaped like trumpets, just the thing for fairies to blow, they are so delicate and pretty. Around the house was a large yard full of trees and shrubs. Outside of the fence stood a row of poplars, as tall and straight as soldiers on guard. There were maples too, and, every autumn, Jack Frost painted their leaves crimson and yellow.

Do you know Jack Frost? He is the merry fellow who pinches your fingers and toes, and the end of your nose and the tips of your ears; and who, to atone for all that, on winter nights draws those beautiful pictures on the window panes for you to look at in the morning. He thinks, perhaps, that you will look at them instead of teasing "mamma" for breakfast. Some of the trees Jack did not paint, but left them green all winter. These were the pines, with their brown cones, and the firs.

How do you like the outside of Frankie's home? The inside was just as pleasant, that is, if any house can be as pleasant as the sky, and clouds, and trees filled with singing birds. The sun came in at the window, where there bloomed scarlet geraniums and heliotropes, and near which a golden canary sang his cheerful songs; and Mrs. Western, Frankie's mother, was so cheerful and good that any place would be pleasant where she was. Frankie's father was in California. It was a sad day when he bade his wife "good-bye," and lifted Frankie in his arms for the last kiss; but he must leave them, to earn money, so that they could keep their pleasant home, for when his factory burned down one windy night, he lost, with it, all his property.

After a few months had passed, Frankie did not miss his father, but played as merrily as ever. What a comfort he was to his mother! So strong, healthful, and happy all the day long! In only one way did he give his mother trouble. He had a very strong will and quick temper, and when he could not have his own way, would sometimes speak hasty, angry words. But his patient mother taught him the wickedness of yielding to his temper, and by gentle words led him to see how dark is the life of sin, and how light and pleasant the "way of holiness."

How Frankie learned to "walk in the light," we shall see from the following chapters.

CHAPTER II.

THE ADVENTURE IN THE CREEK.

"Hurra! hurra!" shouted Ben Field, Joe West, and Willie Prime, throwing up their caps, and giving an extra cheer as they stopped in front of Mrs. Western's gate.

"What are you hurraing for?" asked Frankie, who stood inside the gate, whistling, with both hands in his pockets.

"Coz you've got pants on," said Ben. You wont have to stay in the yard now all the time, just as if you're a girl."

"Don't know," Frankie said, doubtfully, putting his hand on the latch.

"That's right, Frank," said Joe, "come on;

we'll have a game of marbles. I ain't too big
to play with a little fellow, are you, Will?"

Joe was eight and Willie seven years old,
and though Frankie was but six, he *felt* quite
as large in his new pants and jacket, as either
of them; so he said, with an odd little air of
dignity, "I *ain't* a little fellow, and I don't
want to play marbles."

"Of course not," said Willie, "or you'd wear
dresses. I did. I can just remember."

"He had a dress on yesterday, and a sun-
bonnet," Ben said, with a provoking laugh.
"He's growed a lot since then."

"Stop laughing at me, Ben Field. Do you
see my copper toes," and one of the new boots
was thrust threateningly through the fence.

"Never mind him, Frank," said good-natured
Joe. "Come on, boys, let's go to the creek
and wade."

"Don't you want to go too?" asked Willie,
seeing Frankie's wistful look at the mention
of the creek.

"Oh yes!" he exclaimed, delightedly. "Just wait a minute till I ask mamma;" and off he ran, tumbling down two or three times, and rushing into the house like a small hurricane. Not in the kitchen, nor the sitting-room, "Where is mamma?" he said to himself impatiently. At last he opened the parlor door and found her there, fast asleep on the sofa. "Oh dear!" he thought, discontentedly. "Mamma never'll let me wake her up, an' the boys won't wait, an' I can't go." With a sad face he went back to the gate. "I can't go." Mamma's asleep." He put his hands in his pockets, winked his eyes very fast, and began to whistle. All this to keep from crying, and disgracing his new pants by acting like a girl.

"I don't believe your mother'll care one bit. Just to walk to the creek," said Joe.

"No, of course she won't," added Will. "Take off your boots and go barefoot like us boys."

The temptation to go barefooted was too

strong for Frankie, so down he plumped on
the grass, and off came the copper-toed boots
and clean white stockings. In a few minutes
all four boys were running along the dusty
road in their bare feet. It seemed very new
and funny for a while, but after they had gone
half a mile, Frankie began to wish for the cool
shade and moist greensward of home. The
sun burned his head, and the sand of the road
his feet.

"Oh dear!" he said, "aint we most there?"

"Tired a'ready!" laughed Ben. "You're
a great boy. Better go home and sit in mam-
my's lap."

In his sorrowful little heart, poor, tired
Frankie wished most heartily that he was on
his mother's lap that very minute, but he
thought it wouldn't be manly to say so. He
was too tired even to resent what Ben had
said, so he kept still and trudged on.

"I know what we'll do," said Joe. "Will
and I'll make a chair and carry you. And

"WILL AND I'LL MAKE A CHAIR AND CARRY YOU." Page 14.

you, Ben Field, had better keep mighty still, or I'll settle your case in a hurry." For some reason, just then Ben thought best to start off in pursuit of a butterfly.

Joe and Willie made a chair of their crossed hands, on which Frankie seated himself, and put an arm around each of the boys' necks. This mode of traveling pleased him very much, and it seemed but a little while before they reached the creek.

"Ain't it jolly?" said Joe, as he led Frankie into the clear, cool water.

"Oh! oh! see the fishes! the dear little fishes!" said Frankie, stooping to pick them up. But the gay little shiners knew better than to allow themselves to be picked up, even by such a nice little boy. Losing his balance in his attempts to seize one of them, Frankie had a sudden bath in the creek.

"Oh dear! my new pants and jacket!" was the first thing the wet little fellow found breath to say after Joe and Willie had fished

him out of the water and set him on the bank
to dry.

"That comes of bringin' babies along," said
Ben, running down the bank.

That was the drop too much, and Frankie
commenced crying, saying, between his sobs,
'I want to go home. Oh! please let's go
home."

So Joe and Will made a chair again for
Frankie and started for home, leaving Ben to
enjoy his wading alone.

They set Frankie down by the gate, and,
picking up his boots and stockings, he went
into the house.

"Why, Frankie Western!" exclaimed his
mother, as the wet, muddy, rueful little figure
stood in the sitting-room door. "Where
have you been? Your new clothes are ru-
ined." And, carrying the speechless little
fellow into the kitchen, she soon had him
thoroughly washed, and put on one of his
old dresses in place of the new pants and

jacket which were hung up for future atten
tion.

It was a good deal of water for one day,
and the crash towel was rough, and to go back
into a dress and apron after wearing pants,
was something of a trial, but the poor child
was too tired, and too glad to be at home to
care much about it.   After he was dressed he
sat contentedly in his chair till supper-time,
then ate his bread and milk and went to bed.
It was not long before he was dreaming of
fishes and creeks and muddy pants, nor *very*
long before the morning sun drove away the
dreams and opened his eyes.   Jumping up, he
put on his stockings and boots, but pants and
jacket were nowhere to be seen, nothing but
the brown gingham dress and apron.

"Mamma, mamma, I want my pants. Please,
mamma," he said, running into the kitchen
where his mother was getting breakfast.

"They must be cleaned first.   Put on your
dress and come to breakfast."   Her voice was

so pleasant that Frankie forgot his impatience, and dressed himself quickly and quietly.

After breakfast he was about to run out as usual, when his mother said,

"No, Frankie. Mother wants you to stay in the house this morning. She has something to say to you."

"But I don't want to stay, mamma," and he walked slowly toward the door.

"Frankie *must* stay." This was decisive, and he sat down in his chair.

After his mother had finished her work, she took him into the sitting-room, and gave him a seat on a stool by her side.

"Now, Frankie," she said, "I want you to tell me just what you did and where you went yesterday afternoon."

Frankie gave a truthful account of his adventures at the creek. Then his mother said, "Did you know you were disobeying your mother, and, more than that, disobeying God."

"O mamma, I didn't think, I wanted to go

so much," and Frankie looked as though he wanted to cry.

"I know you *wanted* to go, but you must do what is *right*, not what you *want* to do. I will teach you a verse from the Bible that you must remember whenever you are tempted to disobey your mother. It is this: 'Children *obey* your parents in the Lord, for this is right.' Can you repeat it now?"

After a few trials, Frankie could say it without a mistake, and he seemed to understand it, for, when his mother told him that he could run out and play, he put his arms around her neck and kissed her, saying softly, "I'll remember, mamma, that God tells me to mind you."

CHAPTER III.

ALECK—THE NEW FRIEND.

FRANKIE had never been to school, but his mother had taught him to read, and had given him some nice books. These he used to read over and over again until he almost had them by heart. Then, every Sunday his teacher selected a good Sunday School book for him to read during the week. The book she gave him on the Sabbath after his adventure in the creek, was the story of a naughty boy who disobeyed his parents. Frankie read the story with great interest, and did not leave it until it was finished; then, going to his mother, he said, earnestly,

"Mamma, did Miss Campbell know I didn't mind you and went to the creek?"

"I don't know, Frankie," replied his mother. "Why do you ask?"

"Because she gave me a book that tells about a little boy that didn't mind, and ran away to a pond, and got drowned; and I thought she must have known it."

"It may be that she did, but that is of less consequence than the fact that God knows it. Think of it, Frankie, the great and holy God! He sees everything you do, and hears everything you say, and knows all your thoughts.'

"Oh, dear!" sighed Frankie. "I wish he didn't. I never can have any more fun when I think of that. Is he looking at us all the time, every one of us?"

"'Every one of us, and all the time,'" answered his mother. "'His eyes are in every place, beholding the evil and the good.' But that need not trouble you, if you do right."

But I don't do right, you know, mamma, *always*, and I don't believe I can if I try ever so hard. I get tired being good too. I want to play and have fun."

"'Tired being good,' my child. It is the only way to be happy. I know a little boy who is happy all day long, and all he has to make him so, is 'being good.' I am going to take something to his sick mother this evening, and you may go with me."

"Is it the little lame boy, mamma, that lives down by the paper-mill? Oh, won't that be nice! and may I take him one of my books to read?" Frankie asked eagerly.

His mother helped him choose a book, and, after tea, they started. Their way led them along the bank of the creek. The sun was just setting and all the sunset colors were reflected in the water. The hush of the Sabbath was on the busy, noisy village, and nothing could be heard but the faint hum of insects and the good-night song of the birds. Walking by his mother's side, with his hand in hers, all these pleasant sights and sounds around them, and in his heart the thought of pleasing poor, lame Aleck,—all these made

Frankie quietly happy. Looking up into his mother's face, he said, "God is looking at us now, mamma, and I ain't afraid. I wish I could see him too."

"If you love and obey God, Frankie, you will see him, for when you die, He will take you to heaven to live with him forever." This and much more his mother said, and Frankie listened and pondered her words in his childish heart.

At last they reached the widow's little brown house at the foot of a steep, wood-covered hill. It was a "wee sma' place," as widow Espey said, but "didna they hae a' the bonny world outside?"

The sick woman was lying on a clean white bed in one corner of the room. Her face was pale and thin, but the light of a sweet content shone through her eyes. The lame boy, Aleck, was sitting by the bed, his crutches lying on the floor beside him. He had his mother's face, and the same patient, happy look.

"We have been talkin', my bairn an' I, o' the guid land on the ither side," the widow said, after her visitors were seated. "I dinna ken the time, but it wi' nae' be lang before I sha' gang awa' to my 'ain countrie."

Tears came into Aleck's eyes and rolled down his thin, white cheeks.

"Dinna greet, laddie, dinna greet," and the mother stroked his hand that was clasped in hers. "The time wi' be as naething before the guid God wi' ca' ye too, an' we sha' aye dwell thegither. Dinna doot his word, my bairn."

The child bravely kept back his tears and said, "Nae, mither, I ken it wi' a' be for the best; but oh, my ain mither, take your laddie wi' ye," and again the tears came to his eyes.

Frankie's tender heart was touched. Going to Aleck's side, he said eagerly, "Don't cry, little boy. You may have *my* mamma if your mamma dies."

Instantly the dying mother's face brightened, and she said, in faint, earnest tones, "O Mrs.

Western, if ye wad be a mither to my mitherless bairn."

"With God's help I will. He shall be to me as my own child," said Mrs. Western, going nearer the bedside.

"Noo I can gang to my hame wi' a gladsome heart. The Laird wi——." The voice grew fainter, fainter, the breathing shorter. The sobbing child clung about his mother's neck, all the anguish of his soul in the cry, "O mither, mither." The mother's lips moved silently, a glorified look overspread the pallid face, then came the awful stillness. The boy had lost a mother; heaven had gained an angel.

All the sad rites were performed under Mrs. Western's supervision, and, when everything was done, even to the turfing of the last resting-place in the quiet cemetery, the brown cottage was sold, and Aleck was taken to Frankie's home. He shared Frankie's room, and Mrs. Western did all that she could to

lighten his lonely little heart. He mourned
for his mother in a quiet, patient way, but
seemed anxious to be cheerful, and grateful
for his pleasant home and kind friends.

Thus, in the great darkness, the Lord made
his pathway light. "He carries the lambs in
his arms."

CHAPTER IV.

REMEMBER THE SABBATH DAY.

THE sunny summer passed away; autumn came and brightened the hills and valleys for a little time, then was buried beneath its own dead leaves; and now winter has brought its snow and cold winds to Frankie's home.

Frankie loves the winter. The keen winds only make his eyes brighter and cheeks rosier. Then he has such a nice sled, and there are such famous hills for coasting! To be sure, it mars his pleasure to think of Aleck, who is so lame and weak that he has to stay in the house all the time, but he is a merry-hearted little fellow, and dearly loves to go flying down the long hill on his swift-going sled.

"I say it's too bad, Aleck! Can't you *ever* ride down hill?" Frankie's bright face looked troubled. He was buttoning his warm overcoat, to go out for a morning ride.

Aleck's patient face for a moment wore a sad, weary look, then, looking up cheerfully, he said, "Oh, I dinna mind, Frankie,—not much. You ken I'm used to staying i' the house. Then this window is sae sunny, and Dickie sings most a' the time, and the flowers are sae bonny."

"Well, *I* get awful tired when I have to stay in. It's just like having Sunday every day." Frankie gave his fur cap an energetic pull over his eyes, and was starting off with a merry whistle, but his mother, who had been a quiet listener to the conversation, said, "wait a moment, Frankie, I want to talk to you. Why is it that you do not like Sunday? Don't you like to give *one* day to God for all the six working and playing days He gives you?"

"I want to go, mamma. Oh, dear, the boys'll

be gone," was the impatient reply, as he twist-
ed the knob of the half-opened door. "Can't
I go, mamma?"

Mrs. Western said nothing, and, unheeding
her reproachful look, he ran off, drawing his
sled after him.

It was a clear, crisp, sparkling winter morning. Coasting never was better, and Joe and
Will were as merry as ever, but Frankie did
not enjoy it.

"What's the matter, Frank?" asked Joe,
seeing his sorrowful expression. "Fingers
cold?"

"No," said Frankie, "but I am going home,"
and without a word of explanation he ran off.
Rushing into the sitting-room, his eyes filled
with tears, he put his arms around his mother's neck and said, "O mamma, I am sorry."

"So am I, darling," said his mother, kissing
the tearful face. "Sit down here by me and we
will talk a little about the Sabbath, and see
why it is my little boy dislikes it so much."

"I would like it, mamma, only it is so long. I don't like to keep so still, and I get so sleepy in church, and I keep thinking about my sled and the fun I could have if it wasn't Sunday." He paused, quite satisfied that he had made a good case for himself, and his mother, taking up her sewing, told him, in her low, calm tones, the following story.

"A father sent his little boy on a long journey, through a dark and dangerous way; but before bidding him good-bye, he gave him a letter which would tell him how to escape the dangers, and how to find the way through the darkness. This is what he said to the child, who stood all eagerness and haste to be gone.

"'My child, you are just starting on your journey. You are full of life and hope, and the way looks bright before you, but even in this broad, sunny path, are many dangers; and, as you travel further, the path narrows, the flowers are fewer, and the forest is darker; still further on, are rocks, and underbrush, and pitfalls, and at the end of this rough way is a dark and rapid river which you must cross. If you pass over this stream safely, you will find yourself in a beautiful place. In that land I will give you a home, and you shall live with me forever.'

"'But how can I go all that dark way, father?' and the boy's face was full of doubt and fear.

"The father handed him a letter, saying,

"'This letter will tell you just what to do. Whenever you are in trouble, look at this. Nothing can happen to you about which this will not help you. But you are not to travel all the time. Every seventh day you shall pause in your journey to rest and read this letter, and think of all I have told you, and of the pleasant home to which you are going. It will give you so much strength, and make your heart so light and happy that you can travel faster and further than if you had not stopped.'

"'But need I stop at first, father, when the way is easy and I am not tired?' asked the boy.

"'Oh yes, my child, or you will forget it by and by; then, though the way be easy, it has dangers which you cannot avoid unless you study the letter very carefully, and store it in your mind, so that you will know what to do if danger comes suddenly. Therefore, my child, remember to rest in your journey one day out of seven, read this letter, and think of your father and the home beyond the river.'

"Merrily the child started off, chasing the butterflies and plucking the flowers as he ran along the sunny way, so full of glee that he seldom thought of his father's letter until the day of rest came. Then he read it, and tried to think of what his father had said to him; but it was very hard to shut out the visions of the butterflies and birds and flowers. He was restless and tired, for he cared more to please himself than obey his father; so he gradually gave up the day of rest, and then commenced his troubles. All his roses were full of sharp thorns, the path was crowded with rough stones and pricking briers, great snakes darted out from the trunk of every fallen tree, and he grew so weary with constant running, was so bruised with frequent stumbling, and so torn and scratched with briers, that you would hardly have known him. If he had gone on in this way much longer I do not think he ever could have reached the pleasant home which his father was to have ready for him. But in the midst of his troubles he remembered the letter, and, drawing it out of his pocket, read the almost forgotten message, 'Remember the Sabbath day to keep it holy.'"

"That's one of the commandments, mamma," Frankie said. "But was that a true story about the little boy? What was his name?"

"Frankie Western," replied his mother. "God, his heavenly Father, has given him a letter, the Holy Bible, which will tell him

2

how to live every day so as to escape all the
sins that lie in his path, like the stones and
thorns and briers which troubled the little boy.
His Father has told him to leave his work
and play on the Sabbath, and study this letter,
the Bible; but he does not like to do it, and I
fear that in future he will have as much
trouble as did the child about whom I have
told you. He will say more naughty words,
and be more apt to disobey mamma, and to
feel cross toward Benny Field. Then as he
grows older, and the way becomes darker,
I fear he will lose the way and never reach his
home in heaven."

"I don't want to lose the way, mamma. I
won't if I'm good, will I, mamma, and stay in
Sundays, and read the Bible like Aleck?"
asked Frankie, anxiously.

"No, darling, you will not lose your way if
you love God and do just as he commands
you; and one of his commandments is, 'Remember the Sabbath day to keep it holy.'"

CHAPTER V.

FRANKIE TRUSTS IN CHRIST.

ALTHOUGH Frankie was a merry, thoughtless little fellow, his mother's story about keeping the Sabbath made such a deep impression upon his mind that the next Sunday morning his first thought on waking was as to how he should spend the day. There seemed to be a great many hours from dawn till dark, and he sighed half aloud as he thought of the smooth crust of snow and the snow-man left unfinished the day before.

Aleck was awake, and, hearing the sigh, asked what was the matter. "Oh, I was just thinking, Aleck," was the reply, "how long it will be before Monday. Don't it seem ever so long to you? I wish you could go to church with mamma and me. It's nice to hear them sing, but I get sleepy when the minister talks. Didn't you ever go to church?"

"Yes, but I canna remember about it very well. It was before I was lame. But I am sure I wad like to gang to the kirk," said Aleck.

"What made you lame?" Frankie asked, for the first time seeming to realize that his patient playmate had not always been a cripple.

"I fell down the stairs i' the paper-mill where my mither was. It hurt my back some way."

"Won't you get well some time?" asked Frankie, earnestly.

"I dinna ken, but I'm thinkin' 'twill nae be lang till I gang to my mither."

"O Aleck," and Frankie put his arms about his neck, "you mean you're going to die, and you mustn't. You'd have to be put way down in the ground."

"Only my body, Frankie. My soul would be wi' God and my mither. And oh! it is sic a bonny place, and Sunday a' the time. Then I wi' be free frae pain."

"Can everybody go there, Aleck? Am I going too, and mamma, and my papa that's way off in California?"

"Everybody who loves Jesus. If you love him he wi' take you right there when you die. Why dinna you love him, Frankie?"

"I do want to," was the earnest answer, "but I don't know how. I don't believe I love him, or I wouldn't be so naughty."

"The minister at the kirk wi' tell you a' about it, an' your Bible an' your mither, an' if you pray, God wi' help you."

"I will try, Aleck. I'll ask mamma about it, and I'll listen to everything Mr. Price says, and I'll pray too."

Frankie was very much in earnest, and, after he was dressed, he knelt by the bedside, and prayed that God would help him to be good and to love Jesus. On the way to church he talked with his mother, and she tried to lead him to the Good Shepherd. Mr. Price's sermon was written for the lambs of the flock, and was full of encouragement to the little ones to "come to Jesus." Frankie listened with earnest attention to that "sweet story of old, when Jesus was here among men;" his eyes filled with tears, and his heart throbbed at the story of the cruel death on the cross; and when, in conclusion, Mr. Price spoke of the tender love that the Saviour had for little children, and entreated them to give their hearts to him and love him in return, he whispered softly, "I will try to love Jesus."

Frankie was not the only one of the children whose heart had been touched, as the next hour spent in the Sabbath School testified. The teachers sought to deepen the impression, and the Holy Spirit so wrought upon

their young hearts that many went home rejoicing in a Saviour's love.

That Sabbath was a happy day in Frankie's
home. Mrs. Western's heart was full of a
mother's joy over her child, and Aleck shared
in her happiness; as for Frankie, although he
could comprehend but little, he knew that
Jesus loved him, had died for him, and that
he wanted the love and service of just such
little children.   He was but a child, and
would often err, but the hand in which his
was clasped was the same strong hand which
upholds the best and wisest of us all.

CHAPTER VI.

THE FIRST DAY OF SCHOOL.

In the spring, Frankie commenced going to school. Miss Campbell, his Sabbath School teacher, received a dozen little boys and girls at her own house. · They were all nearly of an age and old playmates, so a merry little company they made—full of fun and mischief; but never had school a gentler, lovelier mistress than Miss Campbell, or Miss Ruth, as she wished the children to call her.

The first day of school was as delightful as April sunshine could make it, and Frankie's heart seemed full of sunshine; at least it shone out of his bright eyes, as he kissed his mother, and bidding Aleck good-bye, he ran down

40

the walk, and disappeared behind the poplars. His mother and Aleck watched till the trees hid him from view, then Mrs. Western took her sewing, and Aleck his book. He studied a little each day and always looked forward to the lesson hour with pleasure, but this morning a sigh escaped him as he turned from the out-door sunshine to the in-door work. Full of pity for the patient child, Mrs. Western sat down beside him, and smoothing his hair caressingly, said, "It is hard, my child. I wish you could go too, but your heavenly Father knows best. He does not willingly afflict you."

The tender words brought tears to his eyes, and, resting his head wearily on his hand, he said, "I ken it is a' for the best, I hae a guid hame. You are like my ain mither. The Laird is guid, but I am sae tired."

"You will not feel so tired when you can be out in the air more," replied Mrs. Western, cheerily. "Keep up your courage. You may be a strong, hearty boy yet."

"Please' tell me about heaven. It seems to me it is a bonny country, fu' o' singin birds, and wi' the 'green pastures and still waters;' but I read in the Book that the streets were a' paved wi' gold." The boy's eye brightened as he spoke of heaven.

"'Eye hath not seen, ear hath not heard, neither hath it entered into the heart of man to conceive' the beauties, the glories of heaven," said Mrs. Western; "but this we know, that our Father is there, and that we shall be free from pain, and sorrow, and sin. It will not be long before we shall *know* for ourselves all the glories of that home."

Thus they talked of heaven until Aleck forgot all the suffering and weariness of earth.

Frankie reached Miss Campbell's just in time to get his seat before school commenced. Miss Campbell read a brief chapter in the Bible, and offered an earnest prayer to God, that he would help them to do right and perform all their duties faithfully. Then the lessons were assigned, and they all went to work in earnest. "'New broom sweeps clean,'" said Mrs. Keller, grimly, as she looked in upon them in the afternoon. "Wait a week or so and your hands'll be full. Mark my words, Ruth, those youngones will torment the life out on ye."

Miss Ruth smiled, and looked hopefully at her little charge, as she said, "I don't expect to escape my share of trouble, Mrs. Keller, but I do not think that much of it will come by these little ones."

The children heard the conversation, and mentally resolved to be very good, in order to disappoint Mrs. Keller and to please Miss Ruth.

When school closed they all joined in singing one of their Sunday school hymns— "Let us walk in the Light." Frankie lingered a little after the others went out, and going to Miss Ruth said, "Won't you tell me, please, just what it means to walk in the light? Is it to be good?"

"To be good?" said Miss Ruth "Yes; those who walk in the light of God's commandments are good. But I will explain it. If you were walking alone in the woods on a night so dark that you could not see one step before you, would you not be in danger of falling? And if, in the path, there were deep holes, fallen trees, and tangled underbrush, would you *dare* to walk in such a place on a dark night?"

"No, ma'am," said Frankie, promptly. "I'd take our lantern, and then I guess it wouldn't be so very easy."

"Not *very* easy, perhaps," Miss Ruth replied, "but if in your lantern you had so bright a light that you could see your path plainly, then you could walk around a fallen trunk, separate the tangled briers, and avoid the dangerous holes. With such a journey before you, would you not be very grateful to a kind friend who would offer you such a lantern, saying, 'Take this to be a lamp unto your feet and a light unto your path. If you walk in this light, and trust to me, I will guide you safely through the wilderness into the pleasant land beyond, where you will need no light, and where you will forget all the rough way in which you have come, or remember it only to sing praises to Him who was your Guide and Friend.'"

"Oh, Miss Ruth," Frankie said eagerly, "I know what you mean. The light is the Bible, and the pleasant land is heaven. Mamma once told me something like what you have said."

"Then, Frankie," said Miss Ruth, "remember to 'walk in the light' of God's word."

Bidding his teacher good-night, Frankie went home, his heart full of what he had heard about the "light of God," and of resolutions to "walk in that light."

When he went in he found Aleck watching for him, anxious to hear about the school. So he told him the events of the day, and the conversation he had with Miss Ruth, adding, in conclusion, "and I'm going to try to walk in the light, Aleck. Let us read the Bible the first thing in the morning, before we have a chance to do anything wrong."

"Yes," said Aleck, "and then we'll pray."

"And 'watch,'" added Mrs. Western. "Watch over your thoughts and feelings, and all the little actions of the day. Trust in God, watch and pray, and He will give you the victory."

CHAPTER VII.

THE COASTING MATCH—WHO BEAT?

Miss Ruth found that Mrs. Keller was mistaken; that, instead of being *torments*, her pupils were little *comforts*, and she loved them all very dearly. The spring and summer days flew by, vacation came, and again in the autumn she gathered the children about her.

Much to the annoyance of the little girls, and somewhat to Frankie's, Ben Field had gained admission. "Oh, dear!" sighed Kate Plummer, "that Ben Field is just going to spoil our fun. I can't endure him."

"I do wish Miss Ruth had said he couldn't come," said Lou White, then, tossing back her brown curls, "there's one thing about it, *I* shan't notice him."

47

"Nor I," "nor I," said they all, excepting Millie Ray. Sweet Millie Ray! "Poor Ben," she said, "how lonely he'll be. Don't you think we *ought* to be good to him, Frank," turning to Frankie, who was just entering the school-room. "Don't you think we *ought* to be good to Ben Field?"

"Of course, Millie," said Frankie. "Why? Who isn't?"

"Oh, nobody, only some of us are sorry he's coming to school," Millie answered. "Aint you sorry?"

Frankie hesitated a moment, then said frankly, "No, Millie, I'm not sorry when I think about it as I ought to. Ben needs to come as much as any of us. I guess he'll be pleasant enough if we are good to him."

Frankie's influence gave Ben a better reception from the girls than he would otherwise have met with, and, for a time, he was quite a pleasant playmate. But after a few weeks, when the novelty had worn off, his old spirit of mischief manifested itself. He delighted in teasing the younger boys and little girls.

One day, after the snow came, the boys had a race in coasting, to see which of their sleds was the swiftest. They started at the very top of a long hill. There was Willie Prime on his Reindeer, Joe West on his Express, Ben Field on his Lightning, David Dwight on his Victor, and Frankie on his Light.

They are ready to start. Frankie counts, "one—two—three—four"—and away go Reindeer, Express, Lighting, Victor, and Light. Willie steers too much toward the right, and Reindeer plunges head-foremost into a drift; Joe looks around to see Willie, Express runs off from the track, and both are landed in a ditch on the left. The race is now for Lightning, Victor, and Light; Light being a little in advance, Lightning next, then Victor. Ben is very anxious to win the race. By a push he may turn Light from the track, and thus gain upon Frankie. He steers his sled to the right, and comes down upon Light so suddenly that Frankie is thrown off into the snow, and Victor and Lightning reach the foot of the hill nearly at the same time.

"You ought to be ashamed of yourself, Ben Field! That was a mean trick. I'd play fair if I didn't beat." All this Frankie said, as he brushed the snow from his clothes, and his flashing eyes *looked* every word of it.

"Guess I aint ashamed to beat," Ben said, sullenly.

"But it wasn't fair," said the girls, all in a breath. "You know Frank was ahead till you steered your sled right into his."

"You'd better keep still. I don't want girls meddlin' with my business," said Ben, rudely.

"We are the judges," answered Lou White. "We aren't meddling."

By this time, Frankie had thought what he ought to do. It was hard, but Jesus gave him strength to do it bravely. "Never mind," he said. "Don't say any more about it. Forgive me, Ben, for being angry with you."

Ben *did* feel ashamed then, and the boys and girls looked very much surprised.

"I'd rather not beat than be so mean," Willie said.

"I'd give it to him," said Joe, as he carefully examined Express to see if it was marred by its tumble into the ditch.

"I beat anyhow," Ben said, sullenly, kicking in the snow.

"I think Frank Western beat the best," said little Millie Ray. "Let's judge that Frank beat, girls." So Millie, and Kate, and Lou, and all the girls said that Frankie beat.

"No," said Frankie," "that isn't fair. I *didn't* beat. Perhaps I *might*, but I didn't.

"Just like girls," muttered Ben. "Go for a fellow they like." He walked off, vexed with himself and his playmates, while the others went into the school-room and told Miss Ruth all about it.

Miss Ruth opened the large Bible, and turning to Proverbs, read:

"A soft answer turneth away wrath, but grievous words stir up anger."

"Better is it to be of an humble spirit with the lowly, than to divide the spoil with the proud."

"He that is slow to anger is better than the mighty; and he that ruleth his spirit, than he that taketh a city." Then, turning to the New Testament, she read:

"Love your enemies."

"My little children, let us not love in word, neither in tongue; but in *deed* and in truth."

Miss Ruth closed the Bible, saying nothing, for she knew that the children understood what she had read, and that God's word would reach their hearts better than anything she might say.

They took their seats quietly, and when Ben came in, he was much surprised to meet none but pleasant looks.

When Frankie was on his way home after school, Ben came running to overtake him, all out of breath.

"Hallo! Frank Western, stop a minute," he shouted. Frank waited for him. It was an awkward thing for Ben to do, something he had probably never done before, but he went through with it quite well.

"I say, Frank, that was a mean trick I served you. You took it so cool I was ashamed of myself, and I don't blame the boys and girls for being down on me.

He had not asked forgiveness, but Frankie did not wait for that.

"Never mind, Ben," he said, cordially. "We'll have another race to-morrow. Come home with me and see Aleck. Poor fellow! He gets lonesome." So they walked on together.

"What makes you so much better than the other boys?" asked Ben, abruptly.

"O Ben, don't speak in that way," said

Frankie, looking troubled. "I'm not good, but, do you know, it is ever so much easier to keep from getting angry if you think about Jesus."

Ben looked astonished, but Frankie told him in his own childlike way of the Saviour, and how he would help even little children to serve him.

It was in this way that Aleck and Frankie worked for Jesus, by obeying him, and by telling others of him.

CHAPTER VIII.

ALECK GOES HOME.

WINTER snow gave place to the spring flowers, and now Aleck can go into the yard, with our sturdy Frankie for a support. The boys are together nearly all the time. Aleck, with his gentle ways, to soften the more boyish nature of our robust little hero, and Frankie, with his merry heart, to brighten the life of his suffering friend.

It was Aleck who helped him out of trouble; who urged him to be gentle and forgiving, even to Ben Field; to obey his mother; and to try in every way to please Jesus. It was Aleck who studied the hard lesson first and then helped him, and who sharpened all the slate-pencils; who made the tops and kites and buzz-wheels, and, in short, shared in all of Frankie's play and work.

But as the summer heat came on, the busy hands grew strangely idle. Mrs. Western noticed the change and tried at first by giving simple tonics, then by employing a physician, to restore his strength, but it was in vain. He would lie for hours on a couch before the open window, dreamily watching the soft summer sky, and listening to the singing of the birds.

He seldom roused from this dreamy state, excepting to listen to the reading of the Bible, or to his favorite hymn, "My Ain Countree." Two of the verses he would say over and over to himself.

"The earth is flecked wi' flowers, mony tinted, fresh an' gay,
The birdies warble blithely, for my Father made them sae;
But these sights an' these sounds wi' as naething be to me,
When I hear the angels singin' in my Ain Countree.

"Like a bairn to its mither, a wee birdie to its nest
I wad fain be gangin' noo·unto my Saviour's breast
For he gathers in his bosom witless, worthless lambs
    like me,
An' carries them himsel' to his Ain Countree."

The time was nearer than they thought
when he should go to his "Ain Countree."
Frankie would not believe that Aleck would
die. When his mother told him that it must
be, he ran at once to Aleck, and, throwing
himself on the bed beside him, cried, "O
Aleck, you are *not* going to die. You *must*
get well. Why, you are only two years older
than I am. You oughtn't to die yet."

"Dinna feel bad, Frankie," Aleck said, "I
am sorry to leave you, but I'm glad to be wi'
mither, an' O Frankie, think of it, how
soon I sha' see the Saviour. I wi' wait for
you. You wi' mind a' our talks about Jesus
when I'm gone, Frankie, and try to do something for him every day. There's Ben, an'
Joe, an' Willie, an' a' the lads—tell them
how guid it is to hae sic a friend as Jesus."

"Yes, I will, Aleck. I'll try to do better,

but I won't have you to help me, and it
seems so easy for me to do wrong."

"You wi' hae Jesus. O Frankie, trust
in Jesus."

Thus did the little sufferer, forgetful of self,
seek to comfort others. Very tenderly did
the Shepherd bear this wounded lamb away
from the earthly fold to the shelter of the
heavenly,—so quietly that they knew not
when he died, but thought he slept. In his
sleep he murmured faintly, "Mither," and
again, "Jesus loves me," and a line of his
favorite hymn, "he wi' carry me himsel' to
his Ain Countree." Then came a quiet slum-
ber, followed by that sleep whose waking is
in heaven.

CHAPTER IX.

THE VISIT TO ALECK'S GRAVE. THE FATHER'S RETURN.

FRANKIE missed his friend sadly. He lost all interest in his school, and did not care for kites, or tops, or marbles. He grew pale, and very unlike the once happy little fellow,

> "With eyes so full of brightness,
> And lips so rosily red."

One Sabbath morning in the early autumn he went with his mother to the cemetery. There was as yet no stone at Aleck's grave, but Frankie had planted a white rose-bush, which was then in all its snowy bloom.

"We must take up the rose-bush," said Mrs. Western. "It is an exotic, and cannot endure our severe frosts and snow."

'What is an exotic," asked Frankie.

"A plant that does not grow naturally in our climate. This rose belongs to a warmer climate, and that is why we keep it in the house during the winter. Thus God takes care of his children. Heaven is our home, and when the winds blow too coldly and roughly for us here, God transplants us. He has taken Aleck from all the cold and storms to the heavenly garden. We should nót mourn for him, Frankie. Does not our Father know best? Then it will be only a little while before we shall be taken—only a few years before we shall all be transplanted into the garden of the Lord. You must try to be happy, my child. You must not *forget* Aleck, but remember that you have a work to do for Jesus, and a *part* of that work is to be cheerful and patient, showing that a little boy who loves Jesus need never be unhappy."

Frankie listened quietly. His mother's words made a deep impression, and he tried after that to be cheerful, but it was a long time before his face had its wonted brightness.

Later in the autumn, when the maples were in their gayest colors of crimson and gold, a great joy came to Frankie's home. A letter was received, saying that the father would be with them at Christmas time.

Oh, the preparations that were made for his coming! Frankie worked with his mother, and before winter fairly closed in everything about the house and yard was in perfect order. Then came the waiting, the most difficult task of all. But the even-footed hours will not hurry their pace, so Frankie tries to be patient, and now the day is at hand.

The whole house is made fresh and fragrant with boughs of pine and fir. Only one more night! The father will be at home in the morning.

Frankie thought he would not sleep a wink

for the thought of it, but he did sleep soundly; and when he awoke, the sun was shining into the window; and by the bedside stood his mother, with tears in her eyes, and beside her was the tall man with black hair, and smiling, dark eyes, whom he had seen in his dreams, and whose picture he had kissed and called "papa" even when a baby.

It was indeed a "merry Christmas," and more than that, a joyous, happy one, full of sweet home pleasures and pleasant memories, sanctified by the thought of the dear Christ, God's best gift—his Christmas gift to a sinful world.

CHAPTER X.

CONCLUSION.

FRANKIE was the hero of the school after his father's coming. Boys and girls gathered about him at noon, and recess, and after school, to listen to his stories of his father's life in California—of the giant trees, the mines, the snow-covered mountains, and all the wonders of the Land of Gold.

"Let's go some time, boys," said Joe West, one noon, as they stood listening, with wide-open eyes.

"I'll go," said Willie Prime, "just as soon as I'm a man."

"I'll go before that," said Ben. "'Taint no use for me to stay here."

Poor boy! Having a drunken father, it was not strange he thought it of no use to remain at home.

"Are you ever going, Frank?" asked Millie Ray. "Is it too far for girls to go?"

"Oh no, Millie," answered Frank. "'Tisn't too *far*, but girls would be afraid of the Indians an' bears and everything. But I'l tell you how we'll fix it. We'll all go. Joe, and Will, and Ben, and Kate, and Lou, and you, and I. Then, you know, us boys'll keep the Indians and bears away."

"That'll be splendid," said Millie, clapping her hands as delightedly as though Frankie had been planning a school picnic on the bank of the creek.

The spirit of adventure had so taken possession of the children that they found it very hard to study. Every high snow-bank was the Rocky Mountain range, and every gully or ravine the entrance into a mine.

Miss Ruth had, finally, to insist upon well-learned lessons, under the penalty of being kept after school. Frankie was one of the first to suffer this penalty. He had failed in his geography lesson, having spent his time tracing the overland route to California. Ben Field was the other culprit. It was not new to him, so he cared but little about it, excepting that it pleased him to have such a good boy as Frankie Western kept too.

"How do you like it, Frank?" he asked, as soon as Miss Ruth had left the room.

Frankie had begun to study with all his might, so he looked up only a moment as he said, "I *deserve* it," and after that Ben could not make him speak. Through the force of Frankie's example, Ben also studied faithfully, and when, an hour later, Miss Ruth came in to hear the lesson, both boys recited it perfectly.

It was hard for Frankie to tell his father and mother why he was so late that night, and, for a moment, he felt tempted to give some other reason than the true one; but he thought of what the Bible says of him "who loveth or maketh a lie," and decided to tell the whole truth. It was the last time he failed to study his Geography lesson, but by no means the last time he did wrong. He had the faults and temptations from which none are free, and was but a "babe in Christ," just learning to "walk in the narrow way." But he trusted in Jesus, and tried to imitate his example. The Saviour loves his "little ones" very tenderly, and one of his last commands to his disciples, "Feed my lambs."

In the spring a small marble slab was placed at Aleck's grave, and Frankie set out the white rose bush again, and some lilies of the valley.

The slab had for an inscription only Aleck's name and two lines of his hymn :

"For he gathers in his bosom witless, worthless
   lambs like me,
An' carries them himsel' to his Ain Countree."

Frankie still mourned for his lost playmate and friend; but he was happy in his pleasant home, in trying to please his parents, and in endeavoring to obey his Heavenly Father.

Miss Ruth is still happy in teaching her little ones; Joe, Willie, and Millie have joined in the service of Christ, and Miss Ruth hopes that Kate, and Lou, and even Ben, are *thinking* of what they owe their Saviour. Now we must leave them, rejoicing in the thought that though the world lieth in darkness, in Jesus Christ there is " light for little ones."

THE END.

www.ingramcontent.com/pod-product-compliance
Lightning Source LLC
Chambersburg PA
CBHW022150020726
47496CB00008B/2650